# Crescent Heist

Eric Hua

Published by Eric Hua, 2025.

CRESCENT HEIST

**First edition. April 15, 2025.**

Copyright © 2025 Eric Hua.

ISBN: 978-1069406804

Written by Eric Hua.

# Table of Contents

Thank you to Chelsea for creating all the art in this story.

And thank you Pam for taking the time to edit this story for me.

# Prologue

Hi my name is Gia, and I know this looks really bad, but I promise it's not what it looks like. We are not busting into Santa's workshop. Wait, that sounds horrible, let me restart...

"Aria! What are you doing?! Stop trying to break down that door!"

"Maya is stuck inside! I'm not leaving her alone with those monsters!"

"Okay fine but please, please be..."

(Aria breaks down the heavy door) "Got it!"

"Oh no, that's a lot of angry grimelves!"

"I can take them."

"Aria no don't..." (she runs off to fight alone). "Sigh, why are all the pretty ones so CRAZY!" (clicks a button on her earbud) "Harshitha, anything you can do to help?"

"I relayed your position over, help should be arriving in about...now!"

(A woman wearing a black suit holding two katanas arrives) "Emily!"

"Aria rushed in alone without thinking again?"

"Yeah..."

"Figures. Stay back, I'll deal with this."

"Okay just don't hurt the elves too much..."

(Pause) Alright, this really isn't helping my point is it? Let's start from the beginning.

# Chapter 1: Passcode

It was a Monday morning in the early half of December where the monotone math teacher was lecturing about algebra. After he finished, the students were supposed to work independently on their assignments. Although there were many students off-task, there was one student that the teacher could not ignore.

"Excuse me, miss."

"Yes, Mr. Huackjob."

"Stop talking and focus on your work."

"But Mr. Huackjob, I'm a professional multi-tasker. I can talk and work at the same time! It's quite efficient!"

"Well, in order for me to improve the efficiency of the entire class, I'll have to remove you from this class and have you facing a wall."

"No! Please! I'll focus on my work Mr. Huackjob! Don't move me!"

"Last chance, don't make me regret it."

"Oh, you won't Mr. Huackjob. You won't hear another word from me. No sir!"

As he walked away, her friend that she was talking to earlier wanted to continue their conversation.

"So Gia, who's your Secret Santa?"

"Amaya stop! I can't afford to get in trouble before Christmas. If anything goes wrong and my parents find out I won't get any presents..."

"Oh my gosh Gia there's a spider on your desk!"

"SPIDER?!?! WHAT?!?! WHERE?!?!?!" Her outburst could be heard by everyone including her math teacher.

"Alright class, because you're all being so disruptive, I'm giving you a pop-quiz. You may start when you receive your papers. You have 20 minutes. Good Luck!"

Everyone in the class frantically searched for their school supplies. Gia quickly skims through the test and then flips it over.

"Oh no. IT'S DOUBLE-SIDED!!!!!!"

Skill wise, she was proficient enough to answer all the questions. The only problem was the time constraint placed upon it. It caused her much stress and under the pressure, she was forgetting how to calculate the answers. Before she knew it, time was up.

"Everyone, hand in your papers."

Gia's writing speed increased to a new level but there was no way she could finish on time. Eventually, the teacher walked over and took her test paper by force. Before he let the class go, he had one more announcement.

"Oh, one more thing. This test is worth 50% of your semester's mark."

"WHAT?!" The whole class shouted in uproar.

"Consider it an early Christmas present from me. Have a nice day."

The whole class left dejected, especially Gia. She knew she didn't do well on the exam which meant no Christmas presents for her. She paced down the halls of the school thinking of a possible solution. As she was walking by, she heard a couple of her classmates talking.

"My parents are going to kill me!"

"I'm sure you did fine, Edison. How many questions did you get wrong?"

"One."

"Oh yeah. Your parents are going to make you go without dinner tonight."

"Benji, help me! What am I going to do?!"

"I mean you could sneak in during the night and change out the test."

"Sigh, you're no help. Bye Benji."

"How rude." Benji was about to walk away, but Gia stopped him.

"Benji!"

"Oh hi Gia. This is strange. We usually never talk unless you have math questions during class."

"Benji focus! What were you saying before with Edison?"

"About him not having dinner because he got one question wrong? Don't worry, I don't think your parents are as strict. Are they?"

"Not that!" She looked around and then whispered. "The test papers. Do you know where he keeps them?"

"Oh yeah, Mr. Huackjob keeps them in a lock-safe that requires a passcode to open."

"What's the passcode?"

"Ha, it's not going to be that easy to get me to..."

"Here's the latest math challenge textbook for the elites."

Benji immediately writes the code on a piece of paper for Gia and swaps it for the textbook. He then runs away with glee while Gia stares at the paper given to her, thinking of her next move.

# Chapter 2: Infiltrate

Later that night, after the custodians had finished cleaning the school and everyone had left, Gia began sneaking around the outskirts of the campus. She surveyed the area to ensure no one was around, but then felt a tap on her shoulder.

The person wore a black suit and a mask. Gia was startled and nearly let out a scream, however, the person revealed her face.

"Emily! What are you doing here?" She said in a hushed voice.

"I overheard your conversation with Benji. Figured you could use my help."

"Uhh no offense Emily, I know you are good at math, but how are you going to help me break into the school to get my test paper?"

"Tell me. How were you thinking about breaking into the school?"

"I, umm. I was going to, umm. Use the front door?"

"You haven't got a clue, huh?"

"Okay, you got me. You got a solution?"

"Yeah. Follow me."

The girls snuck around to one of the side doors. The area was well covered compared to the front entrance. However, that seemed to make little difference to Gia as the door was still closed and locked.

"Ugh! What was the point of all that?"

"Well for starters, the school is monitored by the surveillance camera. If you went through the front entrance, you would have been caught."

"Oh, I never considered that."

"Of course you didn't."

"But, it still doesn't change the fact that we can't open this door!"

After saying that, Emily pulled out a ring full of keys.

"How? How did you get those!"

"Let's just say I had a chat with one of the custodians."

"And they just gave it to you?!"

"Yeah, pretty much. I'm pretty good at negotiations."

Emily pointed to her katanas that she had sheathed on her back. Gia had not noticed those until now. She was questioning everything she knew about Emily. The whole image she had of her being a kind and academically strong student was suddenly shattered.

As Gia was lost in her thoughts, Emily unlocked the door. "Hey, I ain't holding this door forever." So she snapped out of her trance and went into the school, following Emily's lead.

Despite having been to the school for quite some time, it was a complete contrast seeing the place during the night instead of the day. With all the Christmas decorations throughout the school in the halls, everything seemed a lot creepier in the dark.

"Gia, are you scared?"

"No, what makes you say that?"

"You've been holding on to my arm the entire time."

"Oh, have I been doing that? My bad." She let go immediately and pretended as if nothing happened.

"Anyway, we're pretty much in our classroom. We just need to open up this door and..."

As Emily unlocked the door, they could see their class Christmas tree with the secret santa gifts below it. However, those were not the only items there. Something grotesque was holding some of the gifts and devouring them at will.

"Uhhh Emily, what in the world is that?"

"I don't know, but it hasn't noticed us yet. Let's slowly walk away and..."

As they were backing up and trying not to make a sound, another one of the creatures was standing behind them. It had razor-sharp teeth and claws, long pointy ears, and it appeared to be wearing a long hat. The beast could smell Gia's fear and it pounced towards her. Gia attempted to run but her legs would not respond. As the creature drew near, Emily pushed it aside.

Despite slamming against the lockers in the halls, it shrugged off the hit and attacked Emily with its claws. Gia was worried until she saw how Emily was able to keep up with the beast's slash with her katanas. It seemed like there might be a chance for them to both get out of this alive. That was until the other creature joined the fray.

With both the creature's combined strength, they pushed Emily back against the wall. She had nowhere to run and her stamina was depleting. The two creatures were slowly approaching their target as Gia looked around for anything that could save her friend. She found nothing, but she could hear footsteps approaching her. Turning the corner of the halls was someone she wasn't expecting to see.

"Mr. Huackjob?!"

"Gia? What could you possibly be doing on school grounds at this hour?"

Immediately Gia went on her knees. "I'm sorry Mr. Huackjob! I tried to sneak in during the night to steal the test papers so I wouldn't get in trouble with my parents! But now Emily is in danger and we need to find her help or else..." She couldn't continue further.

"So you are willing to admit everything you did just to save your friend?"

"Yes! It was all my fault. Please, we need to get help for Emily!"

"Okay." He began walking away from Gia.

"Wait, Mr. Huackjob, that's where the monsters are! Why are you walking towards them?"

"I'll be quick."

"No, don't! You will..." She saw him turn the corner where Emily was and followed him. When she made the turn, she was shocked by what she witnessed. Both the creatures were lying defeated on the ground and Emily was unconscious. "Mr Huackjob, how did you..."

"No time to explain." He began walking away again. "If you want to help your friend, I

suggest you start carrying her and follow me."

Without any hesitation, she grabbed hold of Emily and followed her mysterious teacher through the halls of the school.

# Chapter 3: Spy Academy

Gia was piggybacking Emily as she followed their teacher into the classroom. When the lights turned on, she looked around and found that the room was mostly the same other than for some wrapping scraps on the ground. Her attention was piqued when her teacher moved towards the door at the back of the room. That was when she remembered the rumours that were spread about what was behind this door.

"Mr. Huackjob, I'm sorry please don't put me in there!"

"Hmm?"

"I know that's where bad children go to be tortured and punished. I know what I did was wrong, but please give me one more chance!"

"If you want to save your friend, then you will have to go through this door."

She took a deep breath and then began walking toward the door with Emily still on her back. When she was close enough, the door was opened for her. Instantly, a flash of light blinded her eyes so she covered them as she continued to walk forward. Once she was inside, she could feel she was somehow moving but her legs were still. Looking down she found herself standing on a moving walkway. Then she looked around and saw that the facility she was in looked nothing like her school. Instead, it resembled something far more advanced.

"Welcome to Crescent Spy Academy. Please wait on the auto walkways until you are provided with further instructions." An automated voice said to her through the intercoms.

"Mr. Huackjob, what is this place?"

"Weren't you paying attention to the intercom? Sigh, just like in my math class..."

"Sorry Mr. Huackjob, bad habit." He just shook his head.

Shortly after, the auto walkway ended and presented in front of them was a circular chrome door that required identification to enter. Mr. Huackjob reached out his hand and placed it on the scanning pad near the door. Then he took off his glasses and opened one of his eyes wide for the retina to be scanned.

"Identification complete and access has been granted. Welcome Agent Rice."

"Wait, Mr. Huackjob. YOU ARE A SECRET AGENT SPY?!"

"It won't be a secret for long if you keep yelling it at that volume."

"Oh sorry."

Appearing before them were a couple of agents. "Agent Rice, we heard you had a medical emergency. Are you alright?"

"Oh I'm fine, but I would like you both to take her friend in for treatment." He pointed over to Emily and although Gia was initially hesitant, she handed her friend over to their care.

"We will have her fully operational in no time sir!"

As they left, Gia had some time to let her thoughts sink in. She realized that her once boring math teacher was not as one-dimensional as she thought.

"Daydreaming even when you are out of class?" She snapped back into reality and saw how far behind she was. She ran to catch up onto another walkway.

"Wait, what's going to happen now? Are you going to take me back to school so I can return home?"

"Nope, can't do that."

"What?! Why not?!"

"You have just learned about our secret spy agency."

"I promise I will keep quiet and not tell anyone."

"Like how you keep quiet in math class?"

"Okay, you got me there. So what happens now?"

"Under the strict rules of the agency, I'm supposed to hand you over to the executives who will make the decision and determine your fate."

"No! I'm still so young and I have so much to live for! There has to be another way. I'll do anything, please!"

"Hmm, there might be an alternative."

"Yes! I'll take it!"

"Okay, right this way."

She was led into another room where upon entering, she was met with other people who were her age but seemed very different from her.

"Uh, Mr. Huackjob. What is this? Who are these people?"

"Meet your new teammates."

"Wait, I beg pardon?"

"Starting tomorrow you will be training with these lovely ladies as you are all part of the Crescent Spy Academy!"

"What?! But I never agreed to this!"

"Remember the alternative?"

"Yeah. Wait no, you mean this is it?!" She looked away for a moment but when she looked back, she had lost sight of her teacher. "Hey, where did he go?"

"Good luck with your new team!"

He slammed the door on his way out leaving Gia on her own. Seeing as the door would not open from the inside, she decided to speak with the other girls stuck in the room with her. The first girl she approached had glasses on and was reading her book.

"Hey, what book are you reading?" There was no response. "Umm, excuse me?"

"Oh, were you talking to me?"

"Uh yeah. I was wondering what book you were reading."

"It's about dragons and fairies." She went back to reading.

"So is it good or not?"

"I'll let you know when I'm done." Again she went back to reading.

Realizing the girl's disinterest, Gia turned around, hoping to start a conversation with the other girl. She didn't see one of them and tripped over her as she did that. This one was the tiniest of the girls in the room.

"Hey! Watch where you are going missy!"

"I'm sorry, I couldn't see you as I turned around and..."

"Are you calling me short?!"

"No that's not what I said..."

"Alright, that did it! Nobody calls me that and gets away with it!"

Despite her small stature, she had a fiery attitude which Gia was about to feel. Thankfully, before the situation could escalate, the last girl, who was also the tallest in the room, stood up to defuse the situation.

"Maya, calm down. I'm sure she had no intention of hurting you."

"Hmph, fine." She storms off into her corner.

"Don't mind her, she can get like that sometimes."

"Thanks for helping me out. My name is Gia. What's yours?"

"Mine's Aria. The one who had a short temper with you is Maya. And over there reading the book and ignoring everything else is Harshitha."

"Are they always that friendly?"

"Haha, they just take some time before opening up. Give it some time."

"Okay, I'll take your word for it."

"So what's your covert ability?"

"My what?"

"Covert ability. You know, your special skill or talent that will help you as a spy. Harshitha is extremely proficient in hacking computer systems. Maya is the stealth specialist and infiltrator."

"Then what about you?"

Aria walked up to the wall and took a deep breath before punching it. She leaves a huge dent in the wall. "Brute strength."

Suddenly, Gia had a completely different perception of Aria. Although she was friendly and kind on the exterior, Gia could sense her incredible power. She made a note to herself never to get Aria mad.

"So, what's your ability?"

"I uhh, I don't..."

An alarm sounds throughout the whole facility.

"What was that?!" Gia was startled.

"That signals the end of the day. We all have to head to sleep now so we can be up early tomorrow. Have a good rest!"

Everyone went to their beds and began to sleep. Gia lay there with many questions on her mind. She was still trying to process everything that had happened to her. Eventually, she would be overwhelmed by her thoughts and fall into a deep slumber.

# Chapter 4: Training

G ia woke up to the sound of a blaring horn. It was an alarm that signalled the beginning of the day and could be heard throughout the academy.

"4:00 am?! Who in the world sets an alarm that early?!" Gia yelled.

"Quit your whining and let's go..." Maya said with a grumpy tone.

Together, they all dragged their feet as they got changed and headed towards the training facility.

---

MEANWHILE, AGENT RICE was summoned to the executive meeting room with a panel of five executive members. Unlike before when he was disguised as a math teacher, Agent Rice had a completely different demeanour as he was no longer monotone and stood with confidence.

"Agent Rice, what do you think you are doing?" One voice spoke.

"I just woke up from my nap and I'm planning to go for a walk."

"Don't play dumb with us. You know what we are talking about!" Another voice spoke angrily.

"I do?"

"The five girls!" The third one raised his voice.

"What about them?"

"They are far too young and unskilled to be agents. They must be erased, permanently." The fourth one spoke but was then halted by the leader.

"I'm afraid the council has spoken. The five are to be..."

"Before you make your decision, may I ask, how is the mission going?"

"That's none of your business Agent Rice!" said the final voice.

"Judging by that tone I'm guessing none of the current agents you sent were able to complete the mission."

There was a silence that fell upon the five members before the leader spoke again. "What are you getting at, Agent Rice?"

He held up two fingers. "Two weeks. Give the girls that much time to train and see if they are ready to be sent out on the mission."

"That is preposterous. Some of our elite agents who have trained for years were able to complete such a mission. And you expect some misfit children to accomplish what they could not?" The council members were in doubt.

"How about a wager?" Suddenly he had the executives' interest pique. "I will put my rank on the line. If they are not ready in two weeks, I forfeit my position in the academy and will be expelled never to return."

There was chatter amongst the members. Then the leader spoke up. "Agent Rice, please reconsider..." But the other four members were willing to accept the wager. Therefore, the deal was set and Agent Rice was dismissed from the meeting.

---

"WELCOME AGENTS IN TRAINING. Today you will be tested on your conditioning. You will be tested on your speed, endurance, strength, and mental capacity. Are you ready?"

Aria, Maya, Harshitha and Emily were focused and waiting to start while someone was caught by surprise.

"Wait, I'm confused, what are we supposed to..." Gia asked in confusion.

"Conditioning Training has begun."

The first was speed. It was a hundred-meter dash with Aria, Maya and Emily storming out simultaneously leaving Gia in their dust. Near the halfway point, Aria and Maya were neck and neck until Aria found an extra gear in the final stretch. Aria crossed the finish line with her arms up in celebration with Maya following a couple of seconds behind. Aria thought she had won until she looked at the times on the screen. She saw that she came in second place. Her jaw dropped as she saw Emily sitting alone, having finished before her.

Then there was Gia who barely dragged herself through the finish line. She collapsed to the ground trying to breathe and when she looked up, she saw Harshitha sitting cross-legged reading her book.

"Why didn't you run the hundred-meter dash?"

"I did run it."

"When? I didn't see it."

"I ran it in my mind."

"Hey, that's not fair! I..."

Before Gia could continue, the training simulation told them to progress to the next task. This one would test their mental capacity. There was an explosive in a room and they had to find a way to defuse it before the countdown expired and blew up in the room full of wooden dummies that symbolized trapped hostages.

Emily was first up. She sliced off all the wires on the device but it detonated and she was caught in the explosion. Seconds later, a voice was heard through the intercom, "Detonated, mission failed."

Next was Aria, she tried to punch the explosive but it blew up the room along with all the wooden dummies. "Detonated, mission failed."

Then Maya pulled the explosive out and tried to sneak it out through the vents. However, the explosive was too large and wouldn't fit through the vent. Realizing her mistakes, she crawled through the vents to escape but all the wooden dummies were caught in the explosion. "Detonated, mission failed."

And of course, there was Gia. "Okay, Mister Explosive let's be friends. And as friends, we don't blow anyone up. Sounds good?" A loud boom could be heard. "Detonated, mission failed."

Finally, when it was Harshitha's turn, she quickly assessed the situation. She then connected her laptop to the explosive and quickly typed away with her fingers. Within seconds, the announcement was made. "Explosive defused, mission successful!"

After that, the next task was crawling through a confined space. Maya aced it while the others struggled. In the final event, smashing a brick wall, only Aria succeeded.

At the conclusion of the day, Gia was left lying on the ground exhausted. Harshitha was reading as she left the training facility. Aria was about to check up on Gia but Maya was calling for her.

"Let's go Aria, I'm hungry."

"Oh okay." She looked at Gia, but noticed Emily was approaching her so she left with Maya.

"Hey, how are you holding up?" asked Emily.

"My arms are sore, legs are sore, feet are sore. Everything is SORE!"

"You need some help getting up?" Emily offered.

"No, I need all the help!" Gia whined in response.

Emily was reaching out her hand when one of the agents arrived with an urgent message for her. Immediately she left the room with the agent, leaving Gia behind.

"Umm... Emily? Emily!"

There was no response and Gia had given up on trying to call for help until she heard someone else entering. It was Agent Rice.

"First day and you are already sleeping on the job?"

"It's a miracle I'm not asleep right now. I've been up since 4 am!"

"Well, if you can make jokes like that, you are definitely okay. Better go eat and then rest up. After all, you are going to have to do this all over again tomorrow."

"Hey, before you go. I have something to ask."

"The answer is yes, you need to get all those math assignments done during the break."

"No, not that! I want to ask, why did you bring me here?"

"What makes you ask such a question?"

"I don't know if you saw any part of today, but I'm not good at anything. I'm not fast, strong, smart, and I'm not small enough to crawl through tiny spaces. Did you make a mistake?"

"Perhaps." Agent Rice said simply.

"Wow, that's very encouraging." Gia said dryly.

"The academy rewards those who produce results, not for giving out encouragement."

"Could have at least tried..." She crossed her arms and gave a disgruntled look.

He was about to leave but he paused for a moment. "As for your question earlier, the answer is up to you." He left the room leaving Gia frustrated. Then she realized she was still in the same predicament as before.

"Hello? Is anyone going to help me?!"

# Chapter 5: Simulation

A week had passed with all the girls having shown signs of improvement since they had first begun. They were unaware that they had only a week left to show that they were ready for an extremely difficult mission. So today, their training was about to escalate to a new level.

They entered a room known as the simulation training room. This area could be modified and programmed to create very realistic virtual realities for agents to practice and prepare for their upcoming missions.

"Welcome future agents, here is a mission briefing of your training simulation today. In a few moments, you will see a heavily secured warehouse filled with enemies inside and surveilling the outskirts of the area. There is a valuable item inside that you must secure and escape with. Good luck and remember, work as a team."

Harshitha pulled out her laptop immediately and began typing away. She quickly input all the information she had and her computer was analyzing their best course of action.

"Alright everyone, here is what we are dealing with. Multiple security droids on the perimeter that will prevent easy access from the main entrance."

"Guess you need my help with that," Aria said proudly.

"No Aria, that wouldn't be a good idea. If you take out one of the droids it will just alarm the others. We can't risk that."

"Come on Harshitha, you never let me have any fun."

"So what's the plan then?" Maya asked impatiently.

"Simple. Emily will first sneak her way through which will get her to a control panel that will allow her to open up a small vent on the side.

That will queue you (Maya) to enter through the vents and find the main power room. Once there you will help me disable the surveillance camera and alarm systems. That will only be temporary so in that time, Aria you will have to bust up the door and lock and steal the target item inside."

"Okay, but how in the world do we get out?" Emily asked.

"That's where I come in. While they are busy rebooting the security, I'll temporarily have access to their system and can open up an easy escape route for you without getting caught."

"I get to smash things! Sounds like a good plan to me." Aria affirmed.

"I have no problem with it." Emily also agreed.

"Great, everyone get to your spots and let's begin."

"Umm... What do you need me to do?" Gia asked.

"Uhh, well..." Harshitha was hesitating but Maya wasted no time.

"You can just wait right here; if we need you, we'll call you."

"Oh okay..."

So Aria, Emily, Maya, and Harshitha went to their positions as Gia waited alone.

A couple of the agents running the simulation were watching from above. They were focused on making sure everything was running smoothly. However, one of them ran into an anomaly in the system.

"Hey? You set the difficulty setting to the lowest right?" the first one said.

"Yeah, why?" the second replied.

"It says it's set to the highest difficulty right now."

"Whoa, good thing you double-checked. I don't know how I missed that."

"All good. I'll just adjust this and..."

"What's wrong?"

"It's not working... the setting isn't changing."

"No worries, I'll just reboot the system and... Hey, that's not working either."

"What are we going to do?"

"Guess we just have to let the girls finish the simulation."

"I wish them good luck."

---

AS THE GIRLS WERE GETTING set, Gia waited on a hill from afar until everyone was done with the simulation. She was looking at the ground and having a conversation with herself until she noticed the security drones hovering in the air.

Suddenly, her memories of Harshitha's plan were running through her mind. When she explained on her laptop, Harshitha never mentioned anything about the drones going this far out. Gia then stood up and looked at some of the security droids and noticed their walk patterns also seemed different from what Harshitha's plan indicated.

"Oh no, I have to warn them!" She ran down the hill hoping she wasn't too late.

---

"ALRIGHT, IS EVERYONE in position?" Harshitha asked through the communication device and they all gave her their confirmation.

"Okay, Emily you are up first."

Emily took her time sneaking through the security droids, using her stealth ability and the terrain to her advantage. As she was passing through, she felt it was too easy, sensing there might have been fewer droids, but she proceeded anyway.

"I'm at the panel." she said.

"Okay, I'm transferring the sequence to you now." Harshitha responded.

Emily received it and entered the code on the pad. That opened up a small access to the vent on the side of the building with little to no security in the area.

"Okay Maya, your turn."

"Finally! I've been waiting forever!" She said quietly to herself as she entered through the vent and maneuvered through.

When she got to her destination, she dropped into the room that contained a multitude of complex machinery.

"Uh, what do I do?"

"Don't worry, just place the device where I told you and I'll do the rest."

Maya pulled the device from her pocket and was about to place it where Harshitha indicated. However, the power in the entire place went out prematurely.

"Wait what? What happened? Harshitha? Are you there?" They had lost communication.

"That's weird. I haven't done anything yet. How is the power out already? Maya? Huh?" Harshitha had a bad feeling.

"Hey, Aria something weird happened, you should wait... Aria?" Harshitha realized she could no longer communicate with anyone.

Meanwhile, seeing that the power was down, Aria thought this was her signal. She punched down the door with ease and went through the entrance.

"Hey I'm through, just give me a few minutes and..."

Suddenly the power returned and Aria found herself surrounded by a horde of security droids with all their weapons pointed at her. She was about to turn around and leave but a reinforced chrome door appeared at the entrance and blocked her escape. She had nowhere to run and was left with only one option, to fight.

Elsewhere, Emily was trapped as a fleet of security drones hovered around her. She pulled out her katana ready to defend herself against the nimble and agile flying drones.

Inside, with the power back on, reinforcements were gathering into the room Maya was in. She was forced back into the vents, thinking she could leave the same way she entered. Unfortunately, after making it back halfway, the vent sealed up. She was trapped and to make matters worse, toxic fumes were about to be administered where she was.

# Chapter 6: Operation S.O.F.

F lyer drones surrounded Harshitha. They weren't very powerful but they shot lasers that were stinging Harshitha. The constant attacks were beginning to compound, preventing Harshitha from being able to move.

Gia was running towards Harshitha and could see her comrade under duress. She had to hurry but barding her way were two sentry droids that appeared, each holding a bulky mechanical spear. The twin mechs were far superior to Gia in strength and she had no time to waste. She noticed a small opening between them and took her chance.

She bolted down in between the two sentry guards. The first one swung its spear, which Gia jumped over, and then she rolled away. She continued running and stared down the last obstacle in her way.

The other bulky droid drove its spear, targeting Gia from the front. It was driven into the ground as Gia hopped above it. She landed on the weapon and ran up towards its arm before pushing off its shoulders. She had gotten past the bulky droid and she continued making her way to her ally.

Harshitha continued to cover her head while the flyers continued to attack. She was about to fall unconscious but one of the droids felt a rock clank against its head.

"Hey! Leave Harshitha alone!"

The robotic swarm turned their attention to Gia. She was glad her plan was working until she realized the repercussions of her actions. She turned the other way as she was being chased.

"AHHHH! Why me? WHY ME?!"

The drones were gaining on their target but meeting them on the opposite side were the two sentries that Gia had eluded. They had returned and were ready to trap her. Gia had no other option and was about to give in but Harshitha shouted to her.

"Gia! Keep running!"

"What?! I know you don't like me, Harshitha but can't you get rid of me in a less painful way?!"

"I have a plan, just trust me!"

So Gia put her head down and continued charging towards the twin sentries. They were both prepared to swing their spears. That's when Harshitha called out again.

"Now!"

Gia rolled to the side and the swarm of drones couldn't halt their momentum. Some slammed into the bodies of the sentries. The rest felt the swing of their spears and were no longer operational. The flying drones had all been defeated as Gia laid on her back exhausted. However, the two hulking droids were still functional and had their gaze fixed on her.

"Could I interest you two with the gift of friendship? And maybe a hint of forgiveness on the side?" Gia tried.

They were not amused and were about to attack her. Gia braced herself for the worst but a couple of devices latched onto each of the aggressive robots, which Harshitha had thrown. Once the devices were armed, she pressed a button on her laptop. As a result, the droids' systems malfunctioned. Harshitha let out a sigh of relief but she wouldn't have much time to relax as Gia gave her a big hug.

"Harshitha, you did it!"

"Br..." Harshitha struggled.

"What?"

"Breathe... Need to breathe!"

"Oh sorry." Gia let go. " Thank you for saving me."

After she caught her breath, she spoke. "I should be thanking you. After all, you are the one who saved me. If it weren't for you, I wouldn't be standing here now."

"So what's happening? Where is everyone?"

"I lost communication with them."

"What are we going to do?"

"I... I don't know." A tear was trickling down her face.

"Hey, what's wrong?"

"It's all my fault. My plan failed and now their lives are in danger..."

Harshitha was falling into a dark state, but Gia wouldn't allow it. She grabbed Harshitha's shoulders and shook her.

"Get a hold of yourself! They need your help!"

"Why would they need my help? I got them into this mess."

"Harshitha, do you know how strong Aria is?"

"Huh? Well, yeah. No one in the academy who's fought her has ever won."

"Exactly! And I know Emily is slicing up those pesky tin cans as we speak. Oh, and that Maya is doing everything to crawl out of whatever mess she is in!"

"Everyone... is still fighting." Harshitha realized.

"That's right. They ain't going down without a fight, but they need your help to get them out. What do you say?"

"I'd say, I have a plan."

"Yes! Let's go Harshitha! What are we doing?"

"I'll tell you on the way. Follow me."

"Okay, Operation S.O.F. has begun!"

"S.O.F.?" Harshitha was confused.

"Oh, it stands for Save Our Friends. You don't like it? I can change it if you don't."

"No, it's a great name. Now let's get them back." They were about to make haste but Harshitha had one last thing to say. "Oh Gia, Thank you again."

"Anytime!" Gia replied with a grin.

DESPITE BEING OUTNUMBERED, Emily fought on. She slashed through a multitude of droids using her precision and agility. She defeated the first wave of minions but a lone metallic unit was sent out to fight her. This one appeared different from the rest.

Regardless, Emily attacked the enemy without hesitation. However, the blade could not cut through its armour. She was shocked and was losing her focus. The enemy struck her with an uppercut and she landed with a thud to the ground. She got up and wiped the blood on her lip quickly.

Not wanting to let her recover, the battle droid charged towards Emily. She tried to hold her blades but she felt nothing in her hands. So she glanced around the battlefield and realized that they had been knocked away, out of her reach.

The droid was now standing over her, and she had no way to defend herself. She looked up and noticed a few flyer drones had appeared behind the armoured enemy. Her opponent stood confident as she braced herself for the worse.

The mech was about to land a fierce punch at Emily, but suddenly the drones rebelled and fired their lasers at their ally. The drones' lasers were able to pierce through the armour plating. However, the attacks enraged the armoured droid, so it grabbed one of the flying drones and threw it against another. That created a chain effect as each drone collided with each other and were all defeated.

The armoured droid looked around and found Harshitha standing with Gia. It identified that Harshitha was the one who tampered with its allies. Slowly, it began making its way towards the two women.

"Uh, Harshitha? Please tell me you have another idea."

She threw one of her gadgets at the enemy but it was swatted away with ease.

"I'm afraid I've got nothing."

The droid stopped, then lifted its hand, preparing to strike. The two waited, then suddenly, they saw a katana pierce through the enemy's chest. It was a spot that had been shot by the flying units. The enemy fell to its knees and shortly after, it was no longer moving. Gia and Harshitha looked at the person who had just saved them.

"Emily!" Gia shouted in excitement.

"Hi? Weren't you supposed to be hiding?" Emily was puzzled.

"Plans have changed," Harshitha stated.

"What happened, Harshitha?"

"I don't know. Some of the information we were given was incorrect. I'm sorry to have put you in danger."

"Don't worry about me, I'm fine. What about the others?"

"I haven't been able to reach Aria or Maya, but..."

There was a noise that was heard by all three of them.

"What was that?!" Gia shouted.

Emily traced the sound, "It came from inside."

"Aria! Quick, the gate is just around the corner."

Harshitha led the way and the other two followed. After they turned the corner, they were met with a large metallic gate that was closed. There was also a panel with a number pad that linked to the gate.

"Alright, I'm going to attempt to hack this gate open." Harshitha said as she pulled out her laptop.

"How long will that take?" Emily wondered.

"Ten minutes maybe?"

"Ten minutes?! We don't have time for that!" Gia began pushing random code sequences but they weren't working.

"Gia stop, let me do this. It will be much safer and won't alert any enemy droids."

"Safer?! They already know we're here! We can't lose any more time!"

The two were bickering, but while they were distracted, the gate suddenly began to open. They turned their eyes to the panel and saw that Emily had used her katana to sabotage the mechanism. Gia and Harshitha felt ashamed of how they had acted and apologized.

"Don't worry about that. Just be ready for whatever lies beyond that gate." Emily said calmly.

Gia and Harshitha were mentally preparing themselves for an army ready to attack them. Emily held her katana tightly and when the entrance was fully opened, all three charged in with great fervour. However, once they were inside, all the enemies had been eradicated.

"What in the..." Gia was stunned as she looked around and saw someone sitting atop a pile of droids.

"Aria!" They simultaneously shouted.

"What kept ya?"

"Sorry, the plan didn't go as expected." Harshitha explained.

"That's okay. I managed to get a workout thanks to that."

"Aria, where does it hurt? Did you get hit in the head? What do you need?" Gia asked in rapid succession.

"Gia I'm fine."

While Aria, Gia, and Harshitha were busy chatting, Emily looked at the fallen droids in the room. She began counting in her head but lost track.

"Hey Aria, how many of those robotic tin-cans did you take out?"

She thought for a moment. "Umm... twenty!"

Emily suddenly fell to the ground looking ill.

"Oh my goodness! Emily!" Gia rushed to her side.

"Huh? What's her problem?" Harshitha wondered.

Whispering to herself was Emily. "I only had nineteen..."

As Emily was overreacting, Aria realized that they still had one member missing. "Where's Maya?"

Harshitha pointed to the vents near them. "She should be in there."

Aria walked over to the vent, and using her hands, she pulled off the metal cover. As she did so, a huge whiff of dense air was released, which Harshitha's sensor device picked up on.

"Aria, get out!" Harshitha pulled her friend away to a safer distance.

"What's wrong?" Aria was clueless.

"That vent is releasing a deadly gas. You don't want to inhale that stuff into your body."

Aria was grateful that Harshitha had saved her, but then felt sick when she realized. "Wait, if Maya is in there then..."

"Oh no..." Harshitha caught on.

"I'm going to save her!" Aria was about to rush in, but Harshitha held her back.

"Wait, you can't!"

"Why not Harshitha?"

"Because you are too tall. You won't fit in the vent."

"Oh, good point."

The two were in a dilemma but someone was listening to their conversation. It was Gia.

"I'll go. It's close, but I think I just fit inside the vent."

"No Gia, it's too dangerous." Emily warned.

"And your night time occupation as an assassin isn't dangerous?"

"Okay fair point."

Harshitha scrambled through her pockets before throwing something to Gia. "Here, you'll need this."

It was an oxygen mask that would allow Gia to breathe safely while inside the vents.

"Thank you." She then proceeded through the vent to find Maya.

# Chapter 7: Vent Rescue

T he vent was full of noxious gas that could cause anyone to lose consciousness. Gia could breathe thanks to the mask, but the gas obscured her vision. Luckily, sight wasn't too important as Gia received instructions from Harshitha, who had the vent map on her laptop.

"Take a left, then a right; after that, you should be good."

"Alright Harshitha, thanks, I will let you know when I see Maya."

While Gia focused on covering the rest of the distance, the three girls waited patiently until Gia was finished. All was quiet, which caused them to let their guard down. A red laser dot was meticulously moving and stopped when it lined up with Aria's forehead. She was completely unaware but Emily sensed it just in time.

"Aria, look out!"

Right as Emily pushed Aria aside, a laser beam barely missed them. A squadron of droids armed with high-powered lasers had appeared. They fired their shots at Harshitha, but Emily intercepted them by deflecting the laser away with her katana. She then engaged the enemy and Harshtiha immediately called for Gia.

"Gia, I hate to rush, but you got to hurry. We are under attack..." She cut out.

"Wait, what? Harshitha?!" Gia called back confused.

With no other choice, Gia picked up the pace. She crawled swiftly as she remembered the instructions given by Harshitha. She did everything Harshitha told her, and then stumbled over something."

"Oww... What in the world did I hit?"

She couldn't see initially but once she got a closer look, she noticed it was someone's arm. She looked at the face of the unconscious person.

"Maya!"

Gia checked her airway and was relieved to know that she was still breathing but her heart rate was extremely low. She had a feeling Maya had been exposed to the gas for too long. Using her judgment, she put the mask over Maya and began pulling her out.

Back outside, Emily was doing her best to keep the enemy droids at bay. Aria was about to join the fray but they were about to have another complication. The vent entrance was now automatically closing. Harshitha attempted to hack the system to keep it open, but she didn't have enough time. Seeing no alternative, Aria dashed to the vent and held it from closing with her hands. Although she was strong, Harshitha could see Aria was beginning to sweat. She quickly typed away on her laptop and when she pressed the activation button, a loud sound played from her laptop. She placed it right by the entrance of the vent.

"Come on Gia, hurry!"

Gia continued pulling Maya inside the vent. It was growing more difficult as she had inhaled some of the fumes but she refused to quit. However, she appeared in the path of the vent, which split off and was met with another problem.

"Oh no, which way is it?"

She was struggling to remember but with time ticking, she couldn't just do nothing. She was about to pick a random direction until she heard a loud noise. Upon hearing that sound, she took the path that would lead her to the source.

---

"HARSHITHA, I CAN'T hold this much longer." Aria was struggling.

"Just a little longer! I can see them coming!"

To Aria's relief, Gia could be seen dragging Maya through the vent. There were only a few meters left, but Gia's strength had been sapped. She couldn't pull Maya anymore, let alone herself.

"Oh no, what are we going to do? Come on Harshitha, think, THINK!" She spoke to herself.

"Gia!" Aria called out to get her attention. "Maya keeps a rope on her sash."

Gia mustered her remaining energy and found Maya's rope. She threw one end over to Harshitha, who caught it. Gia held the rope with one hand and Maya with her other hand. Harshitha pulled until both Gia and Maya were near her.

Starting with Maya, Harshitha pulled her out of the vent and then quickly helped Gia after. When everyone was cleared, Aria let go and the vent was sealed off.

Gia, Harshitha, and Aria were lying on the ground, completely gassed. It didn't take long before Maya's eyes began to open.

"What happened? What did I miss?"

Aria, Harshitha, and Gia looked at each other and burst into laughter.

Maya was confused. "You're all crazy. Hey, where's Emily?"

Shortly after asking, Emily was thrown on the ground near them. They were appalled as she had been heavily wounded. There was no way some simple minion droids could beat Emily. However, when they all looked at where Emily was thrown from, they saw a giant mech.

The titan robot was fused from the other enemies Emily was fighting before. It menacingly stood over them and they were astonished by its ability to speak with its robotic voice.

"Foolish spies. You all had plenty of chances to escape. Especially you!" It was directly speaking to Gia.

"You could have been free but instead, you are all captured and will be tortured for information. Do you regret any of your choices?"

Harshitha, Aria, and Maya were silent but not Gia.

"No. I do not regret my choices."

"Oh?" The mech moved to get a closer look at Gia.

"I don't regret my choices. In fact, I would do that again and make sure we all get out of here alive."

"HAHAHAHAHAHAHA!" It was laughing hysterically.

While it was doing so, Aria tried to stand up and fight but her body was exhausted. Maya was still hindered by the noxious gas in her system. Harshitha was out of ideas, and Emily was far too injured. All seemed lost, but something unexpected happened.

"You pass." Said the metallic giant.

As it uttered those words, the mech disassembled. Then, the robotic base they were in became glitchy. Everything was disappearing and suddenly, the girls found themselves back at the spy academy. They were confused, but standing to greet them was a familiar face, Agent Rice.

"Congratulations. You should all go get some rest as your training will resume tomorrow." He was about to leave but Maya spoke up.

"Hey, what happened? We never finished the mission inside the simulation, so why did that robot say we passed?"

The other girls stood by Maya and awaited his answer.

"If you were being evaluated based on what was mentioned in the briefing, then yes, your group failed." All the girls looked defeated. "However, the worst thing you can possibly do is abandon your comrades."

The five girls were shocked as they had never heard him speak in such a serious tone. His attitude at the moment demanded their attention.

"There will always be more missions, but if you lose a comrade on the battlefield, you will regret it forever."

Shortly after finishing his words, he left the area. The girls stayed a bit longer to reflect on what he had said. However, it had been a long day and they were all exhausted. Shortly after, they too left the simulation training area.

# Chapter 8: The Council

Late in the night, Agent Jyles, one of the programmers for the training simulation, was making his way to his room. As he was walking in the empty halls, he noticed Agent Rice in the distance. Jyles was about to call out but he noticed the stern look on Agent Rice's face. He kept watch as he saw Rice enter the Council Room alone. The door closed immediately so Jyles pulled out a device that would allow him to eavesdrop through the wall.

"How can I help you today?" Agent Rice asked.

"Again with the mind games. You can drop the act, because you know exactly why you have been summoned here!" One of the members yelled in anger.

"Oh? Please, elaborate."

"We know it was you who tampered with the simulation system!" Another one accused.

"It is a well-known law that no one can interfere with other agents that are utilizing the training simulation." A different member pointed out.

"I see. So what are you going to do? Am I banished from the academy?" challenged Rice.

"Yes! Exile him!" One of them excitedly said.

However, the leader of the council had other ideas.

"Agent Rice, although your actions didn't cause harm to anyone, you still violated a law on academic grounds. As your punishment, you will be sent on 'the mission' alone."

The other council members were chatting amongst themselves. They knew no spies were able to complete 'the mission' and many worked in groups. They were confident Agent Rice would fail, which was what they were hoping for.

"Well, orders are orders. I can't turn them down. I have no choice but to accept your mission." Agent Rice had no objection.

"You are to leave at once."

Rice was about to leave but the lead council had one last statement to make.

"Oh, we also advise you to keep this mission a secret."

"Yeah, if you mention this to anyone, there will be dire consequences." Another one added.

Agent Rice acknowledged their orders with a nod and walked towards the exit.

Jyles could hear the footsteps approaching in his direction. As the door opened, Jyles panicked and dropped his device. Rice appeared outside, and saw Jyles standing nervously. The young agent was about to speak, but without replying or looking at Jyles, Agent Rice signalled for him to keep quiet.

"What was that noise?" One of the members inside the room asked.

Knowing Jyles would be in trouble if he was caught, Rice improvised. "My apologies, I dropped my watch." He bent down and quickly placed his watch on the ground without the council members noticing. He then picked up the watch for the members to see.

"Tch, clumsy as always, aren't you Agent Rice?"

"It's a work in progress." He smiled back.

The council members were tired of speaking and allowed him to proceed. The door closed and Jyles could finally relax. As he was slowing down his heart rate, Rice spoke to him.

"Pretend you saw nothing, and go back to your dorm." He walked away and disappeared from sight.

Jyles realized that he had been saved from the council's punishment and that Agent Rice was trying to keep him away from trouble. Not wanting to arouse further suspicion, he quietly got up and left the area.

# Chapter 9: The Substitute

The next day had arrived. Although it was another early morning, many of the agents in training were accustomed to the routine now. The alarm sounded and everyone was up to get ready for the day. Entering into the training simulation room last was none other than Gia.

"Sorry I'm late everyone! I ..."

When she arrived, she saw: Aria, Emily, Harshitha, Maya, but there was also someone who she didn't recognize.

"Welcome Ms.Gia, you are late," He said with a monotone voice.

"Uh hi?"

"Now that you are here, your team can finally begin their training." He began to lead them.

Gia immediately ran to Emily with questions. "Emily, what is happening? Who is that?" Emily had no answer but the man overheard Gia's voice.

"Excuse me Miss Gia, it appears you have some questions that I might be able to answer. I'm Agent Dingusberg, your new instructor. I will be overseeing your training for the foreseeable future."

"What about our previous instructor, Agent Rice?"

"I do not know such information. I was only told to be your instructor. Now, enough with the chatter, let us proceed with the training simulation.

The simulation began with the virtual world being created. The setting was similar to before and everyone knew their assignments. Gia, Harshitha, Maya, Aria, and Emily went to their positions.

Harshitha typed away at her laptop while Gia stood near her to relay instructions to everyone else.

"Alright, Emily you're up first!"

Emily snuck through all the droids with ease and got to the control panel. She attached a device to the interface and Harshitha easily hacked the system which turned off the power temporarily.

"Your turn Maya, you got three minutes."

"Easy!"

The tiny spy went into the vent that was unpowered, allowing Maya to move through with ease. She then popped down from the ceiling and landed in a room that had a reinforced side door. Gia relayed the code from Harshitha to Maya. After pushing the sequence, the door opened and allowed Aria to enter.

Together they advanced forward until they arrived at a vault. Maya placed a device on the vault for Harshitha to easily crack. Once the vault was open, Aria went in and saw the relic standing on a podium.

Aria was about to walk forward but Maya stuck her arm out to stop her. Maya then pulled out a spray can and used it to reveal red laser sensors that would have triggered the alarm if any part of their body made contact with it.

After all the lasers were revealed, Maya swiftly manoeuvred her way through to where the relic was. Once she was at the podium, Maya pressed a hidden button on the podium and all the security around the relic disappeared.

Aria grabbed the relic but the power had returned. They couldn't get out the way they came, but dropping from the ceiling were a couple of ropes. Maya and Aria each grabbed one and they were pulled up before any of the security droids knew what happened.

When Aria and Maya got to the top, they were helped up by Emily who stood on the roof. When the relic was confirmed to have left the vicinity of the fortress, the simulation ended.

"Mission complete!" A robotic voice called out.

The virtual world had disappeared and the monotone instructor clapped unenthusiastically. "Well done. You are done for today. We will resume your training tomorrow."

The girls looked at each other confused and wanting further answers. It took awhile, but Maya spoke up for them.

"Hey! Mr. Dingusberg?"

"Yes?"

"What level was that?"

"The first level of course. It's your first class with me so it only makes sense that we start from the beginning."

"So what will we be doing tomorrow?" Aria asked.

"Well, after one is two."

"What?! But Mr. Dingusberg, that is far too easy! We're..." Harshitha yelled.

"You will be training according to the schedule I was given. See you tomorrow." He cut them off and immediately left.

With no reason to stay, the five spies left for the change rooms.

---

MAYA HAD FINISHED CHANGING first and was standing away from the change room door. She was waiting for Gia to leave so she could speak with her alone. However, the more she thought about it, the more nervous she got.

"Hey Gia, how's it going? No, that's too unnatural," Maya thought out loud. "Gia, I want to talk to you about something. No, that's no good either..." she continued. "Okay, just keep it simple and say thank you for saving me Gia."

When she was done rehearsing, she saw Gia leaving the change room. Maya closed her eyes and took a deep breath, but when she opened her eyes, Gia had disappeared. She was confused as to where she had gone, so she left the area guessing Gia went the opposite direction.

In the cleaning supply room near the change room, Gia had been pulled inside by a fellow spy agent.

"Jyles? What are you doing? Are you trying to kidnap me?"

"No Gia, I didn't kidnap you. I have something important to tell you."

"Oh my gosh don't tell me! You are abducting me because you're an alien!"

"What?! No! That's..."

"I knew it! Aliens exist!"

"GIA! STOP! I picked this room because it's one of the few that aren't under surveillance. There's something I need to tell you. It's about Agent Rice."

From there, Gia stopped talking and paid attention to what Jyles had to say. He relayed everything that went on, during the prior night and everything about 'the mission.'

OUT IN THE COLD REGION of the Arctic Circle, a spy jet was flying through the icy blizzard. Piloting the aircraft was Agent Rice, who came to this area alone. He followed the guidance system on the monitor and when he was hovering above the destination, he set the jet to auto-pilot.

He then opened up the back hatch, allowing him to jump out. To slow his descent, he pressed a button in the middle chest area of his suit and glider wings appeared, allowing him to control his drop. He landed on the top of a large warehouse structure.

To cut through the ceiling, he pulled out a tiny gadget that shot out a thermal blade. In seconds, he created an opening and he entered without hesitation.

Once he was inside, he stealthily snuck his way through the area. He arrived in a room where he saw many prison cells occupied by agents from the academy. He lamented at such a sight, but he knew he didn't have much time to act. Using the thermal blade from earlier, he cut through the barrier of the prison cell and grabbed one of the agents who was unconscious.

Just as Agent Rice anticipated the alarm sounded. He began making his way back to where he entered but he could hear a horde of grimelves, running towards him.

Once he arrived at the room he descended from, he pressed a button on his watch, which called the spy jet to hover above the warehouse and drop down a line for him. As this was all happening, the agent he was carrying was waking up.

"Hmm, what's happening? Agent Rice? Is that you?"

"Hi Agent Leo. It is me, but there is no time to catch up or explain. I'm going to send you up to the jet and back to the academy. Find Harshitha and Aria."

"Uhh, okay..." he replied weakly.

Rice then tied the rope around Leo's body and with a press of a button sent Leo up to the jet. However, busting into the room and surrounding Agent Rice was the horde of grimelves. He was ready to fight them all, but appearing out of nowhere was a giant spherical ball that dropped on Agent Rice. He found himself trapped inside an icy prison that was filled with darkness and could not be broken.

He looked at his watch and saw that the spy jet had successfully taken Leo and was making its way back to the Academy. Knowing this, he sat down on the ground getting ready to rest.

"Well, no use in expending my energy. I'll just wait until reinforcement arrives."

# Chapter 10: Sneaky, Sneaky

Inside Crescent Spy Academy was the cafeteria where agents gathered during their break for food and conversations. Many were in line holding their trays containing a plate, a bowl, and silverware. The person at the front was greeted by the lunch lady known as Olivia, who had countless baskets of french bread.

"Bread for you, and you, and you. BREAD FOR EVERYONE!" She gleefully threw them perfectly onto everyone's plate.

After receiving their bread, they moved on to help themselves to some soup and then took a seat of their choice.

Aria was sitting alone, minding her own business, but what she wasn't aware of at the moment was that she was being watched by someone not too far away.

"Okay, to be an incredible spy agent I must master the art of stealth. Identify the target, yes, target confirmed. Mission SAA commence! Now I must be shifty. Right, left, right again, left! Alright, now is the most important part, the element of surprise. She will never see this coming. Initiate plan SAA, SURPRISE ATTACK ARIA!"

After sneaking around the cafeteria and talking to herself, Gia attempted to karate chop Aria. Gia landed a hit right on Aria's left shoulder but Gia was so shocked that Aria didn't even flinch. Instead, Aria turned to look at Gia with an unimpressed facial expression.

"Gia, what in the world are you doing?"

"I was practicing how to be a stealthy agent!"

"I could hear you way before you got near me."

"No you couldn't, I was being sneaky, sneaky."

"You want to see sneaky? Let me show you!" Aria throws a punch at Gia's face.

"Ow! What was that?!"

"It's called a sucker punch." Aria shrugged.

Gia held a hand to her cheek, "How is it even sneaky?!"

"I mean, you didn't see it."

"Argh! Aria!" Gia complained.

Gia jumped on top of Aria and they both fell on the floor throwing hands at each other. They weren't aware, but their fight was causing a crowd to form around them eliciting hollers and cheers as the two went at it.

"Help! Somebody help! Aria is bullying me!" shrieked Gia.

"As if! This kid tried to sneak attack me!" Aria yelled back.

Maya, who was amongst the crowd, snuck through to find the two in a ridiculous mess.

She raised her voice, "What are you two doing?! Cut it out!"

"Tell Aria to stop first!" Gia whined.

"Don't believe her Maya, she started all this!" Aria fought back, slapping Gia's hands away.

As they continued to brawl, security agents began to appear on the scene. They surrounded the two girls and restrained them.

"Alright, break it up, both of you."

The two tried to get one last hit at each other but security held them back. Gia and Aria were led out of the cafeteria separately. Maya pretended not to know them by looking embarrassed. However, little did everyone else know, this was all part of their plan.

WHILE THE AGENCY'S security had their attention focused in the cafeteria, Emily was sneaking her way through the area that contained the agency's database. She peaked over the wall and saw two agents standing guard at a secured door. She created a rattling sound, which got the attention of the two agents.

They walked and turned the corner but found nothing there. While they were confused, Emily dropped from the ceiling and placed a device on both their necks. Within seconds, they fell asleep on the ground.

"Great work, Emily." She could hear Harshitha's voice in her ear piece.

"If we didn't use your device, I totally could have taken them."

"Yeah, but we don't want to hurt anyone from the agency."

"We don't?"

"Emily!"

"I'm kidding Harshitha."

"Quit messing around, they will only be out for ten minutes max!"

Emily refocused and continued moving to where the secured door was. Before getting it to open, Emily pulled out a canister that Harshitha instructed her to throw inside. The door slid open and the canister was rolled into the room filled with a few agents operating the computers. Once the canister hit against one of the operator's chairs, a massive amount of sleeping gas was released throughout the room.

One by one, the agents in the room dropped their heads on their desk. When they were all asleep, Emily walked in with a mask filter on.

Staring at the main computer, Emily pulled out another tool that Harshitha had given her and she plugged it into the computer. From her laptop, Harshitha began hacking the system with ease. That gave her access to the entire agency's database, but she was focused on only gathering what she needed. When she located the desired files, she began downloading everything onto her laptop.

"Alright, it's done Emily. You can get out of there."

Once Emily got the signal, she took the empty canister with her, pulled out the device, and made sure she left no trace behind. After she left, each agent in the room slowly began to wake up from their slumber. They looked around asking each other what happened, but they all seemed too tired to remember. Not noticing anything strange about the room, they went back to work and continued on about their daily routine.

# Chapter 11: Negotiation

Inside Crescent Spy Academy was a hangar that housed all of the academy's aircrafts. It was a well organized system that utilized the space very efficiently and kept the aircrafts in top condition. Specialized agents were allocated the task to make routine check-ups in order to ensure no mechanical issues would be the cause of a mission's failure.

On this night, one of the agents in charge of the inspection was a young girl named Agent Rebecca. Although she was reserved, she was sought out by the academy because of her mathematical talent, work ethic, and attention to detail. Agent Rebecca was in charge of doing an inventory count for the aircrafts in the hangar tonight.

She was going through the motions, as she had done this many times before. However, she came to a halt when something on her checklist didn't comply.

"Huh? Aircraft #X425 has returned?" She went over her papers again. "Taken by Agent Rice. Status: On Mission?!"

She sensed something was wrong and went inside to inspect the jet. Shortly upon entering, she arrived at the pilot seat where all the controls were. She pulled out the history log to find that the aircraft had been on auto-pilot and under stealth mode upon its return. That explained why the status didn't change to inactive.

Rebecca knew that was out of the normal protocol and decided to investigate further. It wouldn't take long as she saw someone lying down, heavily injured. She recognized him from a previous class they had together.

"Agent Leo! What happened? Where is Agent Rice?"

"Ugh... He's... He needs help." Leo was very weak.

"I will report this to the council immediately!" She was about to leave but Leo grabbed her arm.

"No, not them."

"What? But..."

"Get Harshitha. Please, don't tell anyone else."

A COUPLE DAYS HAD PASSED and the council members continued to discuss amongst each other.

"It's been awhile since we heard from Agent Rice."

"That fool is probably a goner, there is no way he could survive."

"But that would mean the mission is still..."

"What should our next move be?"

The four members looked to the lead council who hadn't spoken yet. He was processing the information in his mind until he heard a notification sound on his computer. He pressed the button to receive the call. It was one of the agent's security guards.

"Speak."

"Excuse me sir, but a couple of agents wish to speak with you."

"Who are they?"

"Agent Gia, and Agent Maya, Sir."

The other members all looked at each other confused. They couldn't fathom what the newer recruits wanted. Intrigued, the lead council member told security to let the girls in.

WAITING OUTSIDE WERE Gia and Maya at the door. Further away, hiding down the hall were Harshitha, Aria, and Emily. They wanted to ensure that their two friends got into the council room safely.

"So remind me how we came to the decision that those two would speak with the top heads?" Aria asked.

"Simple. Those two are the best negotiators between the five of us." Harshitha answered.

"What?!" Both Emily and Aria were outraged.

"I could have totally gone for one of them!" Aria yelled.

"Aria, you and I both know that the only kind of negotiating you would get done, is with your fists." Harshitha explained.

"Haha! She got you good there." Emily laughed.

"At least with me, there would still be people to negotiate with." Aria bit back at Emily.

"Okay, cut it out you two! They're going in."

They watched Gia and Maya enter as the door quickly closed behind them. Harshitha pulled out her laptop, and activated a microphone that she placed on Maya, so she could hear the conversation in the council room.

---

"WELCOME, AGENT GIA and Agent Maya. We weren't expecting to see you until your examinations in the upcoming days. How can we help?"

"Sir, we know you have already made plans for our examinations, but our team has a proposition for you." Gia announced.

"How dare you! There are strict protocols and we do not change them under any..." One of the members started in an uproar, but the lead member told him to stop.

"What do you propose?" the lead council member asked.

Maya handed them a file with papers and explained.

"We know about 'the mission' and how none of your agents have been able to complete it."

The whole council tried to hide their disgruntled faces but they could not.

"We also know that you have been trying to get rid of certain agents at the academy. Such as Agent Rice." Maya continued.

"Get to the point!" Another member shouted.

"Instead of having the typical examination, we propose that we take on 'the mission' as our examination." Maya waited for their response.

"Tch, you are in no position to make deals. We can have you expelled for..."

The lower rank member was interrupted by the leader. He was intrigued that they were able to retrieve such information from the academy's security.

"Perhaps I have underestimated your group. Very well, I'll play along. So tell me, if I allow your group to partake in 'the mission,' how do we benefit from this?"

"If we succeed, then you get all your captured agents back."

"And should you fail?"

"You didn't want us around anyways, so if we fail, then you have five less problems to worry about." Maya spoke with confidence.

"You can't possibly be considering this!" One of the council members whispered, but the head council had made his choice.

"Very well, you've got yourselves a deal."

Maya and Gia were escorted to the exit and once they left, the door closed behind them. The two spies were greeted by their teammates, who were relieved they had returned.

"Gia! Maya! You are both in one piece!" Aria was excited to see them.

"How did it go with the council members?" Emily asked.

"It went awesome! We got them to accept the proposal! Well, I didn't do much really. It was mostly Maya who..." Gia didn't finish because she was cut-off.

"It was a team effort." Maya insisted.

Gia looked to Maya for a short second, and Maya returned a smile and winked at her. The two, plus Aria and Emily, were pumped to take on 'the mission,' but Harshitha saw a problem.

"Uh, how are we going to get there?" She asked the girls.

"Can we not just take a cab there or something?" Gia suggested.

"To the Arctic Circle?! Yeah, good luck with that." Harshitha said sarcastically.

"Could we take one of the jets?" Emily asked.

"We are too low rank, none of them are assigned to us. We would need someone of high rank to gain us clearance..." As Harshitha was going through their predicament, someone overheard them.

"I might have a solution to your problem."

"Rebecca! What brings you here?" Emily was excited to see her friend.

She pulled out a piece of paper that had a signature and a stamp of approval. "Agent Rice has granted you clearance to use his jet."

"Well, that was mighty convenient." Maya stated.

"But that still leaves us with one problem. We still don't have a pilot!" Harshitha gave them the bad news.

"I can fly the plane." Rebecca replied calmly.

"Oh, well that just about covers everything then." Harshitha had no other problems left on the list.

"Alright, then it's settled! We are going to fly to the Arc..." Aria covered Gia's mouth and pulled her down back to Earth.

"Gia! It's supposed to be a secret mission!"

"Oh right, sneaky, sneaky. Got it!"

The spies went to pack what they needed and returned to the hanger where Rebecca filed them into the jet. Once they were all on board, Rebecca started the engines. Helping them open the hangar doors was Jyles on the computer. He inputted the codes required, and slowly the gates began to lift open. He also announced through the system for everyone to clear the runway.

When everything was ready and Rebecca was given the signal, she activated the thrusters and the jet took to the skies leaving Crescent Spy Academy behind. The agents were on their way to the Arctic Circle.

# Chapter 12: Air Assault

While Rebecca was piloting the aircraft in the snow, the five spies gathered in a room to discuss their plan. Harshitha had her laptop opened, showing the layout of the building they were about to infiltrate. She went over everyone's responsibilities and possible traps that were inside. When she finished with her presentation, she opened the floor to questions.

Gia was first to raise her hand. "Are we there yet?"

"Gia! You've already asked that ten times!" Maya said, annoyed.

"Actually Maya, she's already at fifteen." Aria had been counting.

"I'm sorry, I'm just very impatient. How about now?"

"GIA!" Maya jumped and grabbed onto Gia.

Aria saw the fight and joined in with the intention of breaking them up. However, her participation only further escalated the fight.

Harshitha was flabbergasted by what was happening. She turned to Emily who sat cross-legged, meditating as if nothing was going on. Harshitha was about to leave the room to find some peace until she heard Emily speak.

"We're being followed."

"What?! Impossible! My laptop would have picked up..." Harshitha was about to check the radar but there was a sudden jolt throughout the aircraft.

Aria, Maya, and Gia were piled on top of one another. Harshitha was picking herself up, holding her head, while Emily calmly stood up. They were confused as to what was going on until the intercom system went online.

"I hate to interrupt everyone, but we are under attack!" Rebecca alerted them.

Harshitha looked outside the windshield. It was difficult to see the enemy aircraft due to it being in stealth mode. However, because of the snow, Harshitha briefly caught the outline of the enemy ships. Again, they fired their lasers and caused Rebecca to pull some sudden manoeuvres.

"Harshitha, please tell me you have a plan!"

"I..."

When she tried to speak, both enemy air units fired their lasers. They struck their target dead-on. Lighting the opposing aircraft wings on fire. It didn't take long before the spy academy ship began spiralling down to the ground.

As the aircraft continued to rapidly descend, part of the jet began to fall apart followed by a couple of small combustions. Eventually, the aircraft crashed into the snowy ground as its parts were scattered around the area.

The two enemy ships that shot down the academy jet landed near the impact. Out of the vehicles appeared a few worker elves with a couple of Grimelves tied to their leash. They were brought to sniff out any survivors from the crash.

The two monstrous brutes were temporarily let off their leash and they were free to find any remains of survivors. As they got close to the broken jet, there was a sudden explosion, blowing up what was left of the aircraft into debris.

One of the worker elves radioed in to report the incident. "The aircraft has been dealt with."

"Were there any survivors?" a voice asked through the radio.

The worker elves made a quick survey of the area and the Grimelves sniffed around without finding any trace of life.

"None to report." The elf confirmed.

"Excellent work. Return to base."

The call ended and the worker elves recalled their two monsters. Once their leash was back on, they all returned to their aircraft. The engines started, allowing them to take-off and leave the area.

THE END?

*Earlier...*

"Harshitha! Please tell me you have a plan!"

"I..."

Harshitha was interrupted as the laser struck the wings of the jet. Everyone was knocked off balance and they slammed against the wall of the aircraft. Although they were in pain, most of them were still conscious, except for one.

"Harshitha!' Aria rushed over to her. She felt relieved when she realized that her friend was still breathing.

"What are we going to do without Harshitha?!" Maya was panicking.

"Gia looked at everyone who seemed confused. She was hoping to find a solution and when she saw Harshitha's laptop on the ground, she picked it up. She opened it and found that it was still operational. That gave her hope to speak to everyone.

"Do you all still remember the plan that Harshitha explained earlier?" Maya, Aria, and Emily all nodded their heads.

"Good, then we just need to find a way out of here." Gia spoke with confidence, which raised everyone's spirit.

"You got any ideas?" Maya asked.

"Not a clue, but maybe Rebecca does."

"Let me go ask her." Emily immediately made her way to the controls and everyone followed after her.

"Rebecca, we need your help."

"Kind of busy trying to keep us alive!"

"Rebecca, is there any way to get out of this jet?"

"Well, there are a few escape pods that can fit two people each."

"What?! Why didn't you tell us sooner?!" Maya yelled.

"Maybe because I'm too busy trying to keep this aircraft from crashing!"

"Hey, it's okay everyone, let's calm down." Gia managed to defuse the situation. "How many escape pods are there?"

"Three."

"If we each buddy up, that'll be perfect!" Aria suggested.

"No, I'll stay on the jet." Rebecca insisted.

"What?! Rebecca, you can't!" Emily refused.

"I need to stay behind to divert their attention. Otherwise, they will pick off each escape pod and this whole mission will fail."

Aria, Maya, and Gia all had a solemn look on their faces. Emily walked up and gave Rebecca a hug.

"Trust me. Everything will be alright." Rebecca reassured her friend.

After the exchange, the agent ran to the escape pods. Aria strapped Harshitha into her seat and then closed the hatch when they were both inside. The second one was boarded by Gia and Maya. The last was Emily's.

On the control panel, there were three bulbs that turned green, indicating the escape pods were ready to be launched. Rebecca told them all to hang on tight as she gripped the controls and focused on what she needed to do.

Rebecca suddenly pulled the emergency brake with one hand and pushed the steering wheel simultaneously. That caused the jet to suddenly dive towards the ground. The enemy fighters immediately followed after them, firing their cannons.

As they were descending, Rebecca spun the wheel and the jet spiraled downward. This caused the smoke on the damaged wings to spread and surround the jet.

"Now!" Rebecca pressed all three buttons to release the escape pods.

The smoke covered the opening of the hatch and the escape pods were released in the sky. The enemy never detected them through all the smoke. Instead, they went after spy academy aircraft and shot it down, slamming it onto the ground.

The enemy units left their fighter jets and were about to check for survivors. However, little did they know, Rebecca initiated the self-destruct sequence before the crash. As they got closer to the aircraft, it exploded, leaving debris scattered throughout the snow.

# Chapter 13: Split Up

A ria was lying on her back as she slowly opened her eyes, finding herself inside what seemed to be a cave. She pieced together that she must have fainted after the escape pod crash landed. She attempted to get up with the little strength she had left, but she felt a rush of pain on her left arm. She applied pressure with her other hand and found that it was wrapped up and held by a sling around her neck.

"How did I injure...?"

"It got sprained from the crash. You are actually very lucky, as it could have been far worse."

"Harshitha! You're okay!" Aria claimed.

She rushed to hug Harshitha. Despite only using her right arm, she was still far stronger than Gia's.

"Aria! Breathe, can't breathe!"

"Oh, sorry about that."

Harshitha took a moment to regain her normal breathing rate before speaking. "Seriously Aria, you will be the death of me someday."

"Heheheh..." She nervously laughed.

"So where is everyone? The last thing I remember was I was talking with Gia and then I woke up inside an escape pod near this cave. By the way, do you know how difficult it was to carry you here!" Harshitha wondered.

Aria explained everything to her teammate that had happened to this point. She also elaborated that everyone was going through with Harshitha's plan that she described on the academy jet. They were all going to travel to their assigned location before executing the plan.

"How's your arm?" Harshitha asked

"Not the best. I don't think it will be much help for this mission." Aria replied.

"No, I meant your other arm."

"Oh my dominant arm? It's good to wallop anything that gets in our way!"

"Alright then, let's get moving. Let's not keep the others waiting."

Harshitha held out her right hand and Aria reached with hers so she could be pulled up. Together, they each activated the thermal mode on their spy suits and made their way out of the cave and through the snow.

IN ANOTHER AREA OF the Arctic Circle, Maya and Gia were making their way towards their destination. The snow was nearly up to their shins. Thankfully, their spy boots and suits were able to keep them warm and dry. They kept walking until Gia saw something faint in the distance.

"I think the fortress is up ahead! Shouldn't be long now!" Gia pointed out, and then continued moving on. As they were making their way towards the fortress, Maya saw this as an opportunity to speak with Gia.

"Hey, Gia, I want to talk to you about something."

"What?! I can't hear you over this wind!"

"I SAID, I WANT TO TALK TO YOU!"

Maya shouted loudly in reply, forgetting her where she was. Her voice had triggered a small avalanche that was heading their way. As it descended, the two, noticing immediately, ran in the opposite direction. However, there was no way they were going to outrun the surge of snow; therefore, they were engulfed by it.

After it subsided, Maya popped her head out from the pile of snow. Slowly, she managed to get herself free without sustaining any injuries.

"Phew, that was a close one. I must be a pretty good spy to get out of that without a scratch. Right, Gia? Uh, Gia?"

She looked around but couldn't see any sign of her teammates. Maya called out Gia's name a couple times but there was no response. Despite that, she was not the kind to give up so easily. She decided to move to a different spot and call Gia again. This time, Maya heard a faint voice. She followed the sound and it led her to a cliff. Maya looked over and saw her comrade had fallen off but was hanging on.

"Gia! Are you okay?"

"Doing great, never been better!"

"Hang on! I'm going to pull you up!"

"Don't worry, I'm not planning on going anywhere."

Maya pulled out a rope from her belt. She held onto one end of the rope and tossed the other down to Gia. Once the rope was lined up to her body, Gia wrapped the end around her waist and gave it a tug, signaling Maya to pull her friend back up.

The rescue was going smoothly as Gia was inches away from returning to the surface. However, the rope suddenly snapped. Gia was about to drop rapidly from a great height.

ALONE IN THE SNOW, Emily held a blank stare. She couldn't accept the fact that she had lost a dear friend. She was hoping the walk towards the fortress along with the freezing temperature would take things off her mind, but it didn't.

With all the walking she had been doing, she knew it would have been foolish to continue. She looked around and found a cave nearby where she could rest.

Upon entering, she quickly found a spot to sit down. However, In her haste, she didn't check the area well enough and the ground beneath her collapsed, causing her to fall. Luckily, the drop wasn't deep and something broke her fall.

She pulled out a small flashlight to see where she landed. It revealed a skeleton, which startled Emily a little. However, as she moved the light around, she found that the place was filled with human skulls, bones, and many rusty, broken down weapons.

Emily knew she couldn't stay, as whatever hunted down these victims was surely still alive. Just as she was about to leave, something was stomping its way towards her. The light was illuminated at the face of the threat; a yeti that stood over a foot taller than her.

Emily looked for options but the cavern beast let out a ferocious roar. She reacted by trying to draw one of her katanas but the yeti tackled Emily, forcing her to drop her weapon. The enemy followed up with a swipe that just missed her. Emily backed away to create some distance but her blade was completely out of reach.

Seeing its advantage, the yeti pressed the attack by charging towards her. It thought its prey was vulnerable but Emily drew her second katana. As they both met in the middle, Emily swung her blade and the yeti, its fist.

They ended up on opposite sides from which they started. The yeti slowly turned around, revealing a cut just above its eyebrow. There was a bit of blood dripping but Emily was not unscathed. She held her abdomen with her left hand.

With the beast unleashing another roar, Emily prepared herself to face her enemy despite her pain. Unfortunately, things were about to get far worse for her as she saw two more yetis emerge behind the one she was already battling.

# Chapter 14: The Yetis

On the outskirts of the fortress, the security elves were found on patrol. Each was responsible for their domain with a bit of overlap to another guard's. Any suspicious activity would be caught and reported by these hard working elves. They were also known for their quick reactions but their skills were about to be put to the test.

One elf in particular was walking his usual route until he stepped on something. He looked down and picked up a gadget that wasn't familiar to him. Then he felt a tap on his shoulder and turned back to find out who it was.

"Sorry to bother you, but my friend accidentally dropped that."

The guard was spooked by Aria's presence and pulled out a weapon, ready to fight her.

"Sigh, guess I have no choice but to take it back by force."

Moments later, another security elf appeared to take his shift. He was expecting a routine work day but then he saw two of his comrades, which was strange. One was lying down unconscious, and the other was an elf who patrolled a different sector.

"What happened here?"

"I'm not sure, I was patrolling my area until I noticed him lying down here."

"I should go report this." The second security elf was about to leave and call for assistance, but then Aria appeared.

"Your friend was not very nice. He took my friend's gadget and wouldn't give it back."

Although taken aback, the two sentry elves drew their weapon and immediately charged at Aria. They thought they could handle their opponent, who was limited to one arm. Despite that limitation, Aria still dealt with her two opponents with relative ease. She also did it without sounding off any alarms.

"How's your set up going?" Aria asked Harshitha.

"It will take a bit more time but this won't mean anything if Maya, Gia, and Emily don't make it on time."

Harshitha was worried about all of them, Aria placed her hand on her shoulder to reassure her friend. "They'll show up. Trust them."

Gia was saved, but only temporarily. Maya's body was near the edge and she was in danger of being dragged down with Gia.

"Maya, you have to let go."

"No, I won't." Maya replied through gritted teeth.

"If you keep this up, you'll go down as well."

"GIA, STOP!" Her response caused Gia to go silent.

"I know you were the one who bailed me out during the training simulation. I'm not letting go because I'm not going to live the rest of my life being in debt to you!"

Because the words came from Maya specifically, Gia knew it was her way of showing she cared.

Gia yielded to her teammate. Maya held on to Gia's arm with both her hands. Then with all her strength, she pulled and threw Gia back to the snowy surface.

"Oh my gosh, I can't believe I just did that." After Maya's adrenaline wore off, she dropped to the snow.

They took a moment to recuperate some of their energy, and when Maya opened her eyes after a short rest, she saw Gia holding her hand out to her. She happily accepted it and Gia pulled Maya back up to her feet. Together, the two continued onwards to the fortress, where they hoped their teammates would already be waiting.

---

EMILY WAS BREATHING heavily as she stood alone facing off against the three yetis. She had lost both her katanas and was left with only her bare hands. Even though the beasts were slow, Emily wouldn't have enough energy to outrun them. At this point, she was completely out of options.

"Guess this is the end of the line. Sorry everyone." She whispered to herself in defeat.

She was about to give in as images of her teammates began to flash before her eyes. First Maya, second Harshitha, third Aria, and finally, Gia. That was the last thing she saw as she closed her eyes. Then suddenly, her mind raced back to when she was in the escape pod. While inside, she saw the explosion of the spy jet that was piloted by her friend, Rebecca. She remembered how powerless she felt in such a situation.

Emily's eyes were now wide open. The vision of losing a dear friend enraged her, and rekindled her fighting spirit. She first stared down the obstacle she was up against and then assessed her surroundings. In that little pause, she had the battlefield memorized and her plan of attack figured out.

The first yeti stepped up, pounding its chest before charging at its target. Emily was currently unarmed but she stood calmly as the beast approached her. As it swung its arm, Emily swiftly dodged to the right. There was a worn out sword impaled to a skeleton that Emily pulled out.

She swung the acquired weapon at the first yeti. Although it wasn't as sharp as her original blades, it still gave the beast a cut on its shoulder.

Seeing its kin injured, the second yeti took charge and attacked Emily. She managed to block the assault but in doing so, had her weapon knocked away. The yeti swung its arm, so Emily rolled to the side and picked up two more broken blades. She counterattacked by slashing the monster twice, giving it two cuts, both on its chest.

Finally, the last yeti ran out of patience. It joined the fray by tackling Emily, slamming her against the wall of the cavern. The lone agent was slow to stand and when she looked up, she saw the three yetis all working together to defeat her.

Not wanting to give her an opportunity to strike back, they attempted to overrun her simultaneously. This situation would have caused many to panic, but not Emily. There were several worn out swords stuck to several skeletons at her disposal. She reacted by picking up one of them and throwing it, landing a hit right at the shoulder of one of the yetis.

Although that briefly slowed down one of the beasts, the other two continued their reckless pursuit. That still did not faze Emily, as she picked up another blade and flung it at the yetis. She did this several times but that didn't completely stop the monsters. Despite suffering many cuts and wounds, they continued to get back up with plenty of energy left.

Seeing this, Emily had one last daring move. She picked up the last broken sword near her and ran straight at her enemies. The yetis were confused but not frightened. They retaliated by charging back, attempting to land a fatal hit.

They all missed the agent as she slid under them. When she saw her opening, she threw the blade, which caused the yetis to split off. That created enough of a distraction for her to reclaim her own katanas. Now, with both her weapons comfortably in her hands, the beasts within the cavern were in for a rude awakening.

She gripped both her blades tightly, then lunged towards her enemies. The yetis thought she had lost her mind, but suddenly, Emily began spinning and eventually created a vortex with her two swords. The beasts were enamoured by the whirling blades and were all struck by the bedazzling attack.

The yetis were lying on the ground separated from one another and filled with cuts throughout their bodies. The smallest one was struggling the most, as it lay on its belly. It looked up and was met with the sight of Emily pointing one of her katanas at its face.

One of the other yetis saw this and immediately jumped onto its kin and gave it a huge embrace. Emily's expression did not change as she was prepared to swing her sword. However, the last yeti crawled its way between Emily and the two defenseless yetis, letting out a weak growl.

Emily paused for a moment, allowing her heart rate to calm down. Now that her mind was more clear, she could see that the yetis were a family. The mother was embracing their son while the father was willing to put his life on the line for the two he cared about most.

Realizing she was the one who intruded on this family's home, she withdrew both her blades. She went on her knees and lowered her head, apologizing to them. Afterwards, she stood up and left the cavern.

On her way out, she still felt the sorrow of losing her friend but she learned not to suppress it. With this valuable lesson learned, she continued on her path to reunite with her team.

# Chapter 15: Impromptu

Much time had passed, as the snowy conditions had subsided into a sunny sky with low temperatures. Harshitha stared at her laptop screen hoping to hear Emily, Maya, or Gia's voice at any second, but time was of the essence.

"Aria, if we wait any longer, our position will be compromised."

"Can we give them just a few more minutes?"

"You've asked that at least seven times already."

"Sigh, you're right. What are we going to do then?"

"I've modified the plan for two people, but the risks far exceed what there were for five. Therefore, I don't expect you to agree to this." Harshitha said unsure.

"What would happen if I decided against this?" Aria questioned.

"Then I would use my other plan: "the solo mission.""

Aria let out a small light laugh. "Ha, as if I would ever leave you alone on an improbable mission."

Harshitha let out a smile before passing a few gadgets to Aria. "Here, you'll need these."

Aria placed the gadgets onto her belt and gave Harshitha a hug.

"You know, there's a high chance we won't make it." Harshitha stated.

"Never know until it's done!" Aria pounded her fists together and then began making her way towards the fortress.

Once she was out of sight, Harshitha went back to her laptop. As she did so, there was a notification on her screen. She clicked and answered the call.

"Harshitha! It's me, Gia! Sorry we are late, but I got Maya here and we are ready to initiate the plan!"

"Oh no..."

"Harshitha? What's wrong?"

"Aria is in trouble! We need to help her!"

"What?! Can you get a hold of her?"

Harshitha tried but Aria had entered into the enemy's domain, rendering their communication devices useless. Both Gia and Harshitha were at a loss for what to do, but Maya spoke up.

"Where is the vent access?"

"They are up on the roofs. Why are you asking?" Harshitha replied.

"Send me the coordinates." Maya requested.

Harshitha typed away with haste as Gia turned to Maya.

"What are you planning?"

"If we carry out Harshitha's initial plan, I might be able to get in through the vents and disable both their surveillance and communication jammers before Aria barges in."

"And what if you don't make it in time?" Gia worried.

"Let's hope it doesn't come to that." replied Maya.

Right as their conversation ended, Harshitha had the coordinates ready. "I sent over the location."

"Thanks, Harshitha."

"Good luck you two."

Their communication devices were now off. Maya and Gia immediately made their way towards the rooftops of the fortress.

Moments later, as Harshitha was anxiously waiting for things to unravel, a notification appeared on her monitor. She thought it was strange as Gia and Maya hadn't been gone for long, so it was unlikely to be them. When she answered the call, she was surprised but also relieved to hear the person's voice.

"Harshitha, I'm here now. My apologies, you would not believe what I happened while I was alone. Harshitha?"

"Emily, everyone's already left to proceed with the plan."

"Oh no, am I too late?"

"No you aren't, but I'm going to need your help soon. Please standby."

"Just let me know when."

# Chapter 16: Breaking In

Aria carefully maneuvered her way into the outer boundary of the fortress. She hid behind cover that was not detected by the surveillance in the area. Slowly, she peaked over and counted four elf guards she would have to face to enter the fortress. She cautiously crept closer so she could make her move.

Meanwhile, two of the guards who were not completely focused on their duties started a conversation.

"So, how did you end up here?" one asked.

Didn't want to get stuck with reindeer maintenance." the other replied.

"No way, you too?!"

"Yeah, I ain't doing that ever again. That Prancer drops a turd that smells nasty."

"Oh yikes. For me it's that one with the red nose."

"Huh? What's wrong with him?"

"I keep trying to take a nap when there isn't much to do, but his nose just keeps flickering on and off!"

"He should really get that checked."

While the two selves were chatting away, they didn't notice that their two coworkers had been taken out until they heard one of them fall over. They were confused as to why one was lying around just before they fully realized what had happened, Aria appeared behind them and with only her right hand, bashed them against each other.

Although she had successfully taken out four enemies, it took her way longer than anticipated because of her injured left arm. She needed to pick up the pace but she heard footsteps running towards her direction. Aria hid behind the wall and when the footsteps got louder, she stuck her arm out and grabbed the enemy. With force, she slammed the guard against the wall. She pulled her fist back, but before her punch could make contact, the person called out to her.

"Aria it's me!" the unknown enemy yelped, taking off her helmet. "See!"

"Gia? What in the...? How did you...?" Aria let go of her.

"Long story. Let me explain!"

*MOMENTS EARLIER...*

Up on the roof, there was one security elf sitting on a chair. He was clearly bored as almost nothing ever happened. The biggest commotions were usually the birds flying over and leaving their droppings behind. Seeing that this was his biggest concern, he moved his chair under cover and began to doze off.

A few minutes later, the guard woke up to find that he was tied to the chair, not only that, he was was also scantily clad. He couldn't get loose and when he looked up, he saw two spies. It was Maya who tied him up and Gia who had stolen his outfit.

"Hey! That's my..." Before he could finish, Maya used a device to shock the man to an unconscious state.

"Phew, that was close!" Gia was relieved.

Maya was now headed towards the vent. Before she was about to head in, she spoke with Gia.

"So you know the plan?"

"Yup, I'm going to find Aria before she breaks in, so she doesn't get caught and then we will go from there."

The two agreed on the plan and split up to fill in their roles. Maya hopped into the vent and pulled up the coordinates on her device. She quietly made her way to her destination, avoiding all security that was spaced out inside the fortress.

She followed the holographic map that indicated where she was until it notified her that the destination was straight ahead. The vent was currently sealed, so Maya pulled out a small laser that could cut through the vent seal.

After the laser finished its job, Maya kicked off the seal and was now inside one of the control rooms. The lone operator heard her entrance and was about to signal the alarm. Maya purposely allowed the elf to do so, and right after he activated it, she threw a device that latched on to the operator, stunning him. Immediately, Maya got on the computer and inserted a different gadget into the system.

Now Harshitha's laptop screen notified her that the enemy's mainframe was available to be hacked. She began typing away, her first goal was to disable the communication jammers. Maya decided to test it out after waiting a short moment.

"Harshitha, can you hear me?"

"Loud and clear! You did it!"

"Good to know. Anyways, I can't chat, I got a bunch of these present wrappers after me."

"I'll send help."

Harshitha replied, but Maya had already disengaged from her device. Immediately, Harshitha turned and nodded to Emily. "You're up!"

---

*BACK TO THE PRESENT time...*

As Gia was speaking to Aria, the alarms began blaring through the fortress.

"What's that obnoxious sound?!" Aria was not pleased.

"Oh no, Maya..." Gia realized what Maya had done.

"Maya is in trouble? We have to go help her!"

"Aria! What are you doing?! Stop trying to break down that door!"

"Maya is stuck inside! I'm not leaving her alone with those monsters!"

"Okay fine but please, please be..."

Aria broke down the heavy door. "Got it!"

"Oh no, that's a lot of angry grimelves."

"I can take them."

"Aria no don't..." She ran off to fight them alone. "Sigh, why are all the pretty ones so CRAZY!" She clicks a button on her ear bud. "Harshitha, anything you can do to help?"

"I relayed your position over, help should be arriving in about... now!"

"Emily!" Gia was excited to see her friend again.

"Aria rushed in alone without thinking again?"

"Yeah..."

"Figures. Stay back, I'll deal with this."

"Okay, just don't hurt the elves too much..."

Emily dashed towards Aria, hoping to quickly assist her. Gia attempted to follow, but someone appeared and blocked her way. The man looked very similar to a figure she heard countless tales about, except he wore a black suit instead of a red one.

"Santa?" Gia called out.

Emily heard Gia's faint voice and turned her head to see the large man towering over her friend. Emily wanted to rush back, but Santa pressed a button and a gate appeared, blocking Emily reach to Gia. She attempted to slash through the blockade with her blades but to no avail. Instead, she was stuck in the room filled with an insurmountable army of elves and grimelves approaching Aria.

WITHIN THE VENTS, MAYA was crawling through, hoping to make her escape. Unfortunately, a grimelf ripped through the upper vent where Maya was, dropping her out in the open area. She slowly got to her feet and saw a squad of security elves standing behind the monstrous grimelf.

OUTSIDE THE FORTRESS, Harshitha was trying to communicate with everyone but no one responded. She attempted to gain access to the surveillance cameras within but her laptop began to react weirdly. It wasn't responding initially and then the screen went haywire. Her stomach dropped as she realized her computer was now being hacked.

# Chapter 17: The Prank

Gia was staring at the figure before her. Everything about his appearance matched the description of the man who spread joy through the world. The only thing throwing her off was the black outfit and his unsettling presence.

"Santa? Is that really you?"

"Yes, I'm the real Santa. But the one you are probably thinking about is my brother, Nicholas."

"What did you do to him?"

"Heh, my brother wanted to do nothing but to spread Christmas cheer throughout the world. He hated people being sad, but he was also delusional. I told him he could not eliminate pain and suffering in the world even for just one day, but he refused to believe me. He wanted to make that one special day happen so badly, that he was willing to overwork his poor elves. So I decided to change things up this year. I thought, why not play a little prank instead."

"And what kind of prank are you planning exactly?"

"A Christmas without any gifts!"

Gia had a flashback of when she snuck into her school to grab the math quiz. The grimelf she saw was devouring the presents under the Christmas tree.

"No! You can't!"

"And who is going to stop me? The Crescent Spy Academy? They are a bunch of fools. I had them figured out a long time ago."

Gia grew curious. "How were you able to capture all those agents?"

"Once I caught the first one, the rest were easy. I was able to siphon information from their minds. Everything they knew about the academy and every other agent was revealed to me. With that knowledge, I easily defeated and imprisoned any agents that dared to wander close to my fortress.

"So that's why no agents have been able to stop you."

"Correct. However, something has been bothering me."

"What's that?"

"There has been little to no information about you or your team. Your group has gotten further than the more experienced agent squads. So as a mastermind I must know, who is the one behind all this?"

"I don't know what you are talking about."

"Let's try this again. You can tell me right now, or I will extract that information from you myself. Either way, I will have my answer. One will be much less painful." The dark Santa threatened.

Gia remained silent. Seeing as he was not going to get what he wanted from her, Santa reached out his hand, ready to extract the information he needed.

---

IN A DIFFERENT ROOM, both Aria and Emily were breathing heavily. While they were trying to catch their breath, a couple of grimelves attacked Emily. She was able to fend off one of them but the other one bashed her to the ground.

"Emily!"

Aria was appalled by the sight of what occurred. She attempted to help her comrade but a chain was wrapped around her right arm. The security elf pulled the chain and Aria fell to her knee. As she was restrained, a small group of enemies slowly approached to capture her.

Emily was slow to get up as she used her katana for support. She could see Aria in a dire situation, but her own wasn't much better. Grimelves were walking her way and it seemed to be the end of the line. However, Emily caught a glimpse of the grimelf she defeated earlier.

The slash left a cut on the chest of the beast, showing its electrical circuits had been damaged.

Emily threw one of her katanas that missed all the grimelves approaching her. None of them were her target, she was aiming for the security elf that was holding the chain that restrained Aria. The blade pierced the elf's heart and revealed that it was a robot as well.

The security elves inside the fortress were not like the ones Aria encountered outside. This meant Aria no longer had to hold back. She swung her right arm that still had the chain wrapped around it. Using it as a temporary weapon, the chain whipped aside a large chunk of the enemy forces.

With her enemies dealt with, Aria picked up Emily's katana and threw it back to her teammate. The swordwielder caught her blade and slashed aside the remaining grimelves. Emily and Aria had survived but multiple hatches began to open up. Enemy reinforcements had arrived. The two spies stood back to back as they stared at the endless waves of enemies.

"Want a rematch?" Aria asked.

"It won't be fair, you have an injured arm." Emily rolled her eyes.

"Are you scared then?"

"Pft, as if." Emily fell for the taunt.

"Alright then, don't lose count!"

Together, they readied themselves for their final stand as they counted their own knockouts.

MAYA WAS ALONE, FACING against the one grimelf and the mass of elf droids. The grimelf charged at the little agent, who reached for her rope. The creature pounded the ground but Maya sipped under its legs. She then climbed on the monster's back and tied the rope around the grimelf's jaws. She now had temporary control of the beast.

Maya pulled on the reins and the grimelf ran around, swinging its claws wildly. The mechanical elves that were caught in its path were swept aside. Things were going well, until the beast ran into a wall, knocking Maya against it and dropping her to the ground. The impact had hurt her shoulder, but more importantly, the beast was freed. It stood with the remaining minions, wanting revenge on the little spy.

WITH HARSHITHA'S LAPTOP under the contamination of a virus, she pulled out her tablet. This device also had access to the enemy's mainframe and Harshtiha could think of only one last option that could possibly save everyone. As she rapidly worked on her screen, she hoped everyone was still hanging on.

TRAPPED WITHIN A LARGE globe prison was Rice. His eyes were closed and his body was resting until he heard a static sound. The security system of the globe was faltering thanks to Harshitha's efforts. He stood up from his nap and touched the barrier, which no longer delivered electrical feedback. He pulled out a device, which made an exit for him.

Once he was freed, he looked around to see he was in the jail where there were a multitude of cells. Each of them contained an agent from the academy. Slowly, each lock was being disabled and there were no guards left in the area because they had all been alerted to deal with the intruders.

Seeing this opportunity, Rice checked on some of the agents and gathered as many of them as he could who were still able to fight.

# Chapter 18: Merry Christmas

Gia was pressed against the wall by Santa who held his hand out, ready to extract the information out of her mind. She continued to struggle so he decided to snap his fingers. Multiple screens turned on and they revealed Gia's teammates nearing their own demise.

Aria was holding her injured left arm, while Emily was reduced to only one katana. They slowly backed away from the mass of approaching enemies until they hit a wall.

"So, how many did you get?" Aria asked.

"Thirty." Replied Emily.

"Darn, I only had twenty-five." Aria replied feeling bummed.

"Wow, you still kept it close despite fighting with one arm." Emily said, trying to console her.

"It ain't over yet." Aria said glaring at her teammate.

"Ha, that's what I thought you would say."

The girls still had their fighting spirits despite their energy being nearly depleted. The army of grimelves and elf droids were ready to strike, but they halted their advance when they heard a mechanical sound; it was one of the gates lifted up, revealing a group of freed Crescent Spy Agents. They held up weapons they found throughout the fortress and they charged at the enemy to assist the two female agents.

The sight of reinforcements rejuvenated both Aria and Emily. They were willing to re-engage the battlefield, continuing their contest.

Santa was now frustrated after seeing what was happening on the screen. He shifted his attention to the other, hoping for a different result. However, what he saw was something similar. Another uproaring group of agents that rallied to help Maya out of her predicament. That left only Gia.

"No! This can't be happening!" He turned to face Gia. "You distracted me this whole time!"

Gia waved nervously. "It wasn't on purpose."

"Argh! Enough! No more distractions! I will end you once and for..."

He felt a tap on his shoulders. Santa turned around and saw Agent Rice waving at him.

"I know this will probably put me on the naughty list but..." Rice threw an uppercut that landed on his opponent's jaw, dropping him to the ground. "Merry Christmas."

"Agent Rice! You're okay!"

"You sound surprised." Agent Rice replied.

"But you were captured, and everyone was in danger, and, and..."

"Hey, it's alright. You did very well. Everything went according to plan."

Santa was slow to get up but he overheard their conversation. "You... It was you!"

"Hmm?" Rice pretended to be confused.

"You were the one behind this!" Santa complained.

"I might have helped a little." Agent Rice said with a shrug.

"You knew it was futile to be sending agents that were highly experienced with a long history with the spy academy. That's why you sent these girls instead, didn't you?"

Rice smiled and didn't say a word, allowing Santa to continue. He realized the agent's plan went further than he initially realized.

"You even got yourself captured on purpose! Argh!" He had enough of talking.

The man was growing far too furious with each passing moment. In his rage, he was about to attack both the agents but a reindeer appeared and tackled him to the ground. There was a rider on it, who hopped off. When Santa looked up, he had the look of fear in his eyes.

"Brother! I... What are you doing here? I was only..."

"That's enough from you!" The large bearded man with a white outfit snapped his fingers and a squad of elves appeared. "Arrest my brother. I will deal with him personally."

The elf complied and immediately handcuffed the dark Santa with candy cane coloured handcuffs.

"No! Stop! I'm sorry I gave you those cookies and milk laced with sleeping pills! It was all just a prank! You know me. All jokes!" His voice faded away as he was shoved in a giant toy bag and thrown onto the sleigh.

After his brother was taken care of, the man turned to the two agents. "My apologies for the troubles my brother has caused everyone."

"What's going to happen to him?" Gia asked.

"Rest assured, he will be punished severely for his crimes." He got onto his sleigh that was tied to his reindeers. "Oh, and Merry Christmas!"

The reindeers all moved in unison when he took control of the reins. They disappeared into the sky and all the mechanical elf droids ceased to function. Gia was about to relax, but walking towards her were some familiar faces.

Maya was slowly limping her way while Harshitha appeared after. They were about to speak with one another until they saw Aria, who was being supported by Emily. When they were all assembled together, Agent Rice spoke.

"Well done agents, you have successfully completed 'the mission' and saved Christmas for everyone."

"That's great and all, but how are we going to get out of here?!" Maya sounded agitated.

"No need to worry, she's got us covered."

After Rice replied, Rebecca appeared in front of them. "I already notified the academy. They are sending a rescue fleet for everyone here."

Everyone was shocked to see Rebecca but none more than Emily, who rushed over to give Rebecca a big hug. Rebecca! You aren't a ghost! It's really you!"

"Of course it's me!" Rebecca replied.

"My brain is trying to comprehend how this is possible..." Harshitha was going to have a headache.

Rebecca began to explain what happened back on the spy jet.

Right after she released the escape pods, she stayed inside the aircraft to initiate the self-destruct countdown. Once it started, Rebecca pressed a button, which allowed part of the jet to disassemble into a much smaller aircraft. Rebecca activated the stealth mode and flew away, while the larger body of the spy jet crashed. When the countdown hit zero, the jet self-destructed, destroying any evidence of her escape.

"Ow!" Emily smacked Rebecca on the head.

"Don't you ever scare us like that again!"

Maya, Aria, Harshitha, and Gia couldn't help but laugh. Shortly after, they could hear many aircrafts hovering above them. The rescue crew had arrived to help everyone return back to the academy safely.

# Chapter 19: Departure

About a week later, the majority of captured agents had made a full recovery. To celebrate, a large party was held at the academy. Of all people, Olivia was in charge of providing food. No one ever went hungry because there was bread for days.

Throughout the building, everyone was enjoying the event. Agent Jyles was speaking with Agent Leo about their favourite animated shows. Emily and Rebecca were trying to get Olivia out of food duty but Olivia refused. Agent Maya decided to provoke Aria by throwing a slice of bread at her. The bread had jam on it, leaving Aria's suit with a massive stain. Aria grew furious and ran after the little agent.

Then there was Harshitha, who was minding her own business, reading her book. She was enjoying another one of her adventure novels when she heard footsteps approaching her. Without losing her pages on the book, she responded.

"No Gia, I'm not in the mood to join in right now."

"Oh that's okay, I understand. I was actually here to ask you about something else."

She put her book down. "What is it?"

"Have you seen Agent Rice?"

"Knowing him, he's probably hiding somewhere. He'll show up when he wants."

"Okay, thanks Harshitha."

Gia was going to walk away while Harshita was returning to her book. However, Gia stopped for a moment.

"Oh, Harshitha."

"Yeah?"

"What you did back at the Arctic Circle was nothing short of amazing!"

Harshitha was stunned. No one had said anything to her about that until now. "Thanks Gia, I appreciate it."

Gia returned to Emily and Rebecca, while Harshitha re-entered her world of adventure.

INSIDE THE COUNCIL room, Agent Rice stood alone with the council members seated around him.

"Tampering with the training simulations, acquiring classified information without permission, giving inexperienced agents access to a highly specialized vehicle, and operating alone without reporting to the council." One of the members read out.

"Agent Rice, these are only a few of the codes of conduct that you have broken." Another member announced.

"Your actions can not be overlooked, and your punishment will be severe." The third added.

"However, your plan did save many lives, including some who we know personally." The fourth member spoke.

Now, the final council member was about to reveal the decision to be made. "Agent Rice, the council have discussed much and we have come to a conclusion. We have decided that you are to provide 200 hours of community service. In addition, you will be kept under close surveillance for the foreseeable future. Do you have any final remarks?"

"I do." He placed a letter along with a badge, in front of the leader.

"You... are you leaving the academy?!" One of the members was shocked.

"Isn't that what you always wanted? To get rid of me?" Rice replied.

"You insufferable fool! After we decided to keep you around!" Another member shouted angrily.

The lead member held the rest back from speaking. "What will we tell the students about your sudden disappearance?"

"You can let everyone know that I was expelled for not following the spy academy conduct."

"Very well, if that is your decision, I will accept. However, because this is considered a banishment, you are to leave the academy grounds immediately without a word to any of the agents."

"Understood. Thank you for all your efforts, Council Members." He then left the room without bumping into a single person in the academy.

THE NEWS OF RICE'S departure was not announced until the next day. Although a detailed explanation was given, many rumours still swirled around, but no one ever found out the real reason.

The night before, when everyone was finished celebrating, all the agents returned to their rooms. When Maya, Aria, Harshitha, Emily, and Gia were about to lay down on their respective beds, they each saw a letter with their names on it. The agents picked it up and opened the contents. What they saw was a math quiz that each one of them had been given before becoming a spy. On the paper, they saw in bold capital letters, 'FAIL!'

"WHAT?!?!"

They were all in outrage until they flipped to the back side. He was only joking and went on to indicate that they had exceeded his expectations.

## *The End?*

# Concept Art

By: Chelsea Wang